A Beautiful Life

Life

Una Vida Bella

A VENEZUELAN MIGRATION STORY

SHARLENE ANDREWS-ALEXANDER

The Velasquez family along with many other Venezuelan nationals entered the seaport in Cedros, south Trinidad, on a boat called, 'Vida Bella', which translated means beautiful life. It was symbolic of the life that they all expected to have in Trinidad and Tobago. Mr. Jose Velasquez, wife Isabella, their son Juan and their daughter Sofia, excitedly disembarked from the boat and entered the Immigration Building to begin the immigration process. After one hour, the Velasquez family walked out of the Immigration Building to begin their beautiful life in Trinidad.

"Jose Velasquez! Back to work, your break is over!" barked Mr. Roberts, the owner of the poultry farm where Jose worked.

Jose's body jolted back to the present time as he snapped out of his daydream. He got up and unhurriedly walked back to scrubbing the poultry pens. Jose shook his head, remembering his life in Venezuela as an engineer. He was shocked by how he had transformed to a lowly labourer, a far cry from the prestigious job back home. He was also aware that due to the immigration laws in Trinidad and Tobago, that he could not work legally. At that thought, he quickened his pace as he realized he was grateful for the job he had and knew his family depended on him as the breadwinner.

Meanwhile, Isabella pounded the pavements in the Cedros community looking for a job. She tried several businesses, but none of them had anything available. She even tried cleaning homes, but no one would allow her to bring her daughter Sofia to work with her. Sofia was four years old, but she was not as lucky as her older brother Juan, who had gotten into a primary school. So, Isabella had to find a job that allowed Sofia to be with her even when she went to work. Back home, Isabella was a lab technician, and here in Trinidad, she couldn't even find a job as a cleaner. She wiped a stray tear as she walked sluggishly around the community in her quest to find a job.

Later that evening, Isabella and Jose put the children to bed and decided to have a heart to heart conversation about their lives.

"Jose, I walked all over the community today and I still couldn't find a job. I even offered to clean people's houses, but I couldn't find anyone allowing me to take Sofia. I am running out of options," said Isabella sorrowfully.

"I know, I am getting tired of working on the poultry farm. While I am grateful for the income, I have a problem with the way the owner speaks to me, as if I am dirt. As well as the fact that the salary is so small. It can barely take care of our needs. We need to come up with a new plan," replied Jose.

Isabella said, "Let's think about it over the next few days and then we'll discuss it at the end of the week."

"Sounds like a great idea," said Jose as they retired to bed.

Jose always took time to update his family in Venezuela about his family's life in Trinidad and Tobago. He would write letters to them, as the cell phone service was sometimes unreliable. One night, when everyone was asleep, he wrote:

Dear Family,

I hope this letter finds you all in good health and in safety. Isabella, Juan, Sofia and I are doing well. Not as well as we would like, but we are alive and well. I have gotten a job on a poultry farm tending to the chickens and cleaning the pens. It is a lot of hard work and I do not get paid much, but it's enough to put food on the table.

Juan has gotten into a school, but Sofia is still too young to get into a primary school here. We have to wait until she is five years old. Juan had some issues at school, but they were sorted out and he is thriving well now. Isabella has tried to find a job here in the Cedros area but was unsuccessful since she has to find a job that allows her to take Sofia along. We hope things would get better. Please pray for us as we continue to pray for you and our beloved country. I will communicate with you soon.

Love Jose.

A few days later, husband and wife continue their discussion.

"Jose, I think we should move to another part of the country. Cedros is too small and I need to find a job to help the family," indicated Isabella.

"I think that is a good idea, but we will have to move Juan to another school. You know that could be a problem as not all schools take Venezuelan children," replied Jose.

"Any ideas where we should move to?" questioned Jose.

"I think we should move to central Trinidad. I heard some people saying that they saw many Venezuelans in central and they even have Venezuelan children in the schools," answered Isabella.

"Let's take a drive up there tomorrow and look around," said Jose.

The next day, which was Sunday, Jose hired a taxi and together with Isabella and the children travelled up to the central area.

They drove around looking for a place to rent and for help wanted signs. While the driver was driving, Isabella kept her eyes opened for apartment rental signs, while Jose scoured for 'help wanted' signs. They checked a few apartments, but the rent was too high. Finally, they were able to locate and secure a reasonable, small, two-bedroom apartment to rent and they got a few telephone numbers to call for jobs.

While driving along Munroe Road, they stopped at a Chinese Supermarket called Wing Lee's Supermarket to purchase snacks for the kids. While shopping, Jose happened to see one of his secondary school classmates, Luis Rodriguez. They embraced each other and started conversing in Spanish. Jose introduced his wife and kids to Luis and explained to him what they were doing in the area.

Luis heard the frustration in his friend's voice and decided that he should try to help.

Luis asked to speak to the owner Mr. Lee, he told him about Jose's plight and Mr. Lee offered to give Jose a job working in the supermarket as a stock clerk. Jose eagerly accepted the offer as it would have been a step up from the poultry farm. Luis also suggested several schools within the area that were accepting Venezuelan children. The family enjoyed the blissful ride back to Cedros realizing it was the happiest they had felt in a long time.

Isabella and Jose packed their meagre belongings the next day and hired a van to take them to their new home located in the Charlieville area. Upon arrival, the driver and Jose unpacked the heavier items, while Isabella, Juan and Sofia unpacked the lighter items. They set about quickly arranging their new apartment. It was not much as both Sofia and Juan had to sleep on the same bed in one of the bedrooms, but they were comfortable.

The following day, Jose reported for duty at Wing Lee's Supermarket. Luis was his immediate supervisor. Luis showed him around and told him what his duties were. Jose set about completing his tasks with a smile on his face and a spring in his step throughout his shift.

Isabella, on the other hand, eagerly worked on enrolling both Juan and Sofia into a school. Isabella was lucky to get Juan into a denominational school within the area, but Sofia was still too young for a primary school. She visited some pre-schools in the area, but many of them were filled. The last pre-school she tried however, was an Early Childhood Care and Education school and they agreed to take Sofia. Isabella was on cloud nine. Once both children were in school, she could then look for a job to contribute to her family's needs.

The next day while Jose was at work, Isabella set about acquiring the school supplies that both children needed to begin school. This dipped heavily into their small savings, but it was necessary. She thought that the savings would be built up again once she started working. Isabella did everything to ensure that both children could begin school the next day.

The following morning, Isabella woke up bright and early to prepare the children for school. Sofia moved a bit slowly as she was unaccustomed to getting up that early. Isabella made a mental note to put Sofia to bed a little earlier in the evening to help with this issue. Both children were ready by 7:30 a.m., and Jose was tasked with the responsibility of dropping them off at school. Isabella packed both lunch kits, hugged and kissed both children as well as Jose, and they were out the door. She then quickly got herself ready to go job hunting.

Isabella needed to get a phone card to make calls to the numbers they collected the other day, so she walked down the street to the corner shop. While on her way there, she passed a construction site. As she passed the site, the workers who were on a break started heckling her about her beauty.

"Darlin'!" shouted one worker.

"Lookin' good!" yelled another.

"Hola senorita!" called out yet another.

Isabella gave an awkward, polite wave and continued on her journey.

When Isabella arrived at the shop, she had to wait in line as there were a few customers ahead of her. As she got to the counter, she asked for a fifty-dollar phone card. The customer who was chatting quietly with one of the shop keepers, upon hearing Isabella's thick Spanish accent, stopped in mid-conversation and swung around to face Isabella.

"Ah next Venezuelan again?" yelled the female customer.

"All yuh Vene woman only comin' here to take people man! Ah tired ah all yuh! Why all yuh doh just go back to Venezuela?" shouted the customer.

The shop keeper grabbed her hand to calm her down.

Isabella got red in the face. She quickly retrieved her card and beat a hasty retreat out of the shop. She walked quickly back to the apartment and shut the door. Isabella then proceeded to make phone calls. She was successful in setting up some interviews for the next few days, which she attended with no positive feedback. Many of the employers wanted to see her work permit, of which she had none. Isabella felt disappointed and sad but kept attending the interviews. The last interview she went on, she had her hopes up expecting to get the job, but her hopes were dashed when the employer stated that she was not what they were looking for. Isabella felt so crushed that she slowly walked along the street looking for a taxi to head home. While waiting for a taxi, she felt thirsty and reached into her bag for her bottle of water, only to realize she had forgotten it in the office where she had the interview.

She looked around for a place to purchase a bottle, but the only place available was a bar. She really wanted the water, so she walked into Tipsey's Bar. While waiting to be attended to, she looked around and spotted a 'help wanted' sign for an attendant at the bar. Isabella purchased the bottle of water and enquired about the job. She spoke with the manager, Mr. Adams, who was very pleasant. They talked for a while and at the end of the conversation, Mr. Adams offered Isabella the job.

"Gracias, gracias senor!" (thank you, thank you sir), was Isabella's response. She was smiling from ear to ear and was scheduled to begin work at the beginning of the following week.

Isabella decided to make a celebratory meal for the family to celebrate her new job. She made a chicken salad arepa (a corn cake which is split open and filled with avocado and chicken) and batido (a fruit juice which is thick in texture and made with more fruit than water). While Isabella was preparing the meal, she flipped on the radio.

Josephine: This is Josephine Gibbs, and you are listening to the programme Focus on the Nation here on Radio 100.9 f.m., bringing you the trending topics in the country. Welcome back to our program. If you're just joining us, with me in studio is our resident psychologist, Dr. Franny Francis. We continue the conversation about the Venezuelan explosion in Trinidad and Tobago.

Dr. Francis, before the break, one of our callers expressed the thought that many Trinbagonians have shared, that they do not want Venezuelans in our country. This caller was extremely passionate about this. Is there a name for what this caller is experiencing?

Dr. Gibbs: Yes Josephine, this feeling is called xenophobia. Xenophobia is the unreasonable fear and dislike of foreigners. Josephine, this fear can become evident when nationals of a country become suspicious of foreigners and their activities. Nationals may be afraid that non-nationals may want to take their jobs and by extension they may believe that the foreigners want to take over the country.

Josephine: Before we move on to the next caller Dr. Gibbs, are there any practical steps which can be taken to decrease xenophobia?

Dr. Gibbs: Excellent question Josephine, there are several steps that can be taken to help alleviate these feelings:

Social media can be used as most people are on several social media platforms. This can be used to bring awareness to the concept of xenophobia and promote messages of peace and tolerance. This can be done by governmental agencies or through NGOs or faith-based groups.

Public forums can be used. A panel of learned individuals, such as psychologists, immigration officers and members of the protective services, can have meetings in public spaces to share ideas and experiences and shed light on this issue. The public can also gain an opportunity to air their concerns and have them addressed.

Also, public awareness campaigns on television, the newspapers and the internet can also be used.

Media personnel can also highlight the plight of the Venezuelans. Letting the public see the human side of these refugees.

Josephine*: Great ideas Dr. Gibbs. We're off to another break and we'll continue our interesting conversation when we return.*

Station ID plays in the background.

Jose and the children came through the door. The children rushed to kiss Isabella and head off to their room to put down their bags. Jose also puts his bags down and kisses Isabella.

"Something smells delicioso! (delicious in Spanish). What's the special occasion?" enquired Jose.

"I got a job!" answered Isabella excitedly.

"Yay! Yay!" cheered the children.

"Felicidades!" (congratulations in Spanish), shouted Jose happily, as he gave Isabella a kiss.

Jose and the children were delighted when Isabella placed dinner on the table. They had not had this special meal for a long time.

"Where is this new job?" asked Jose.

"At Tipsey's Bar in Curepe," said Isabella.

"A bar?" yelled Jose.

Jose's mood changed from joy to anger.

"I do not want my wife working at a bar. You need to look for another job. No wife of mine is going to work in any bar, with all those crazy characters!" replied Jose adamantly.

"Jose, remember I've been on several job interviews before, and many employers were asking for my work permit. I do not have one, so I could not have gotten those jobs which were much better. This is the only one I got since we arrived here, let's give it a chance. Besides, Mr. Adams is paying me thirteen dollars an hour. This is just two dollars short of the minimum wage. Please Jose!" implored Isabella.

Jose thought about it and agreed. He was getting paid even less than that per hour. He agreed to allow Isabella to work at Tipsey's, only if she promised to be extremely careful. Isabella agreed.

Isabella began work and she really enjoyed going to work and interacting with people. She had worked for two weeks at Tipsey's and she was proficient in her job and she was even making tips. One day, a rowdy bunch of customers came into the bar. Isabella was their attendant. They ordered a round of drinks and some food. They talked and laughed loudly in the bar. Mr. Adams had to ask them on several occasions to tone it down. Isabella served them quickly and with a pleasant disposition. When she went to deliver the third round of drinks, one of the customers grabbed her butt which made her scream out in shock. Mr. Adams, who was close enough to have observed the situation immediately reprimanded the customer and all the members of the group. He then took over the service of the group and apologized profusely to Isabella, assuring her that type of behavior rarely occurred at the bar. Isabella thanked Mr. Adams for his kindness and she continued her work.

Things were going well for the Velasquez family. Everyone was doing well and thriving in their new environment. Jose sends another letter back to Venezuela.

Dear Family,

I trust this letter meets everyone in safety. We are all doing great over here. Things have started looking up for us. We have moved to a new apartment in Charlieville and both Isabella and I have found jobs. Isabella is working in a bar and is making good money with her salary, as well as tips. I am working in a Chinese Supermarket and I am being treated fine. Both Juan and Sofia are in school and excelling in their studies.

The government of Trinidad and Tobago would be making plans very soon to register Venezuelan nationals on Trinidad and Tobago soil. Registered Venezuelans would be given a card with a photo and some basic information. This would allow us to work in the country between six months to a year. Registration allows some aspects of public healthcare. There is no guarantee of access to education. This process will provide some benefits to Venezuelans as well as prevent employers from taking advantage of Venezuelans. This would help our country-men out tremendously.

I will communicate with you soon.

Love Jose.

A few weeks later, Jose received a letter from his mother. He went into the bedroom to be alone to read the letter.

The letter read:

My dear son,

I hope this letter finds you and the family in good health. We are doing the best we can to survive over here. Things are still difficult, but the money you have been sending makes it a little easier.

Juanita is trying to find a job to help the family, but it has been hard. No one seems to be hiring at this time. She is getting restless. She and I had a discussion recently and we decided it would be best if she comes to Trinidad to stay with you for a while. She can get a job; she can be part of the registration process and work to send money home. I can no longer work and prices of everything goes up by the day and items are still scarce.

I know that I would miss her help around the house, but your brother Diego has agreed to help as best as he can. I gave her some money that I was saving for my medicine to buy the ticket, which she bought yesterday, and she would be arriving next week. I would have Diego call you with the day and time of her arrival.

Please kiss Isabella and the children for me. May God bless us all.

Love,
Mama Rosa

Jose did not realize there were tears in his eyes as he read the letter. He closed the letter, closed his eyes, smelt the letter and kissed it as if he was kissing his mother. Jose felt sad because he missed his mother and brother, and even though his homeland was in turmoil, he missed his country; he missed home. Jose wiped his tears and went to tell Isabella and the children the news, and to prepare for Juanita.

A week later, Jose made the journey to Cedros, at the same jetty he and his family arrived only a few months before. It brought back memories of how they were both nervous and excited on their arrival. He waited outside the Immigration Building for Juanita. Jose spotted her as she alighted from the building. As she made her way towards him, Jose assessed his sister. He thought that she looked a bit thin, but he was excited to see her. They both embraced and conversed rapidly in Spanish. They then boarded the taxi that Jose had hired, and they were off to the apartment.

Juanita drank in all the sights with her eyes and the quiet ride was punctuated with little squeals ever so often when she saw an interesting sight as well as rapid conversations in Spanish. By the time the duo arrived home, it was dinner time at the Velazquez home. The children did not want to eat their dinner until their aunt arrived. As the door cracked open, both Sofia and Juan rushed to the door to greet their aunt, whom they had not seen for months.

"Hola tia," (hello aunty in Spanish) both children shouted as they grabbed Juanita.

"Hola mis hijos," (hello children in Spanish) replied Juanita as she bent down to hug and kiss both the children.

Isabella made her way to greet Juanita, while Jose took her bags to the bedroom. Isabella and Juanita embraced and kissed each other. Isabella held Juanita's face in her hands as they conversed rapidly in Spanish. They chatted about all that was going on in both Trinidad and Tobago and Venezuela. The family then sat down to their dinner.

Juanita settled into her new environment for the first few days before she started looking for a job. One evening, while at the dinner table, Isabella revealed to the family that her boss, Mr. Adams, had an outing organized for his workers and their family the next Sunday. She told them that he did this twice a year to bring his employees and their families closer together. Everyone at work was really excited about it, as they were heading to Maracas Beach. Isabella expressed her interest in attending as the family had not been able to see any of the sights of Trinidad since they arrived. Jose also expressed his interest in going and it was decided that the whole family would be attending the outing. Everyone was really excited.

The day of the outing arrived, everyone got up early and readied themselves for the trip. They left home extra early to arrive at the designated meeting point. While they were waiting for transportation to arrive, Isabella introduced her family to all her co-workers. A little while later, several maxi taxis arrived, and everyone entered and settled themselves for the ride. Sofia and Juan sat together as well as Isabella and Jose. Isabella sat in a double seat just behind the children, so she could keep a close eye on them. Just as their maxi was about to leave, a young man excitedly entered the maxi and settled right next to Juanita. He placed his things down, turned and greeted his colleagues then turned to Juanita and introduced himself.

"Hi, my name is Marlon," as he stuck out his hand towards Juanita.

Juanita shook his hand and introduced herself. "My name is Juanita," she said shyly.

Marlon and Juanita chatted all the way to Maracas. The maxi taxis stopped along the Maracas Lookout and people were able to come out and stretch their legs as well as sample some of the indigenous delicacies. Some people used this opportunity to take pictures of the breath-taking sight of the ocean. Jose spoke with the vendors and purchased some red mango, sugar cake and paw paw balls for Isabella and the children. They were excited to try them.

"Daddy, what are these green balls called?" asked Juan.

The vendor responded, "There are called paw paw balls. Made from the paw paw or papaya fruit."

"Yummy, these are delicious," exclaimed Sofia excitedly.

"What do you have mama? asked Juan.

"I have red mango," replied Isabella.

"Can we try some?" inquired Sofia.

Isabella gave some to Juan, Sofia and Jose.

"Wow, this is lovely," replied Juan.

Meanwhile, Juanita and Marlon were busy sampling the delicacies. Marlon bought items such as fudge, bene sticks and pineapple chow for Juanita to sample. They were engrossed in sampling, talking, laughing and getting to know each other. They also took some pictures together. It was then time to board the maxi taxi to head to the beach.

A few moments later, the maxi taxis headed down the incline, and the beach became visible. All the children were delighted and began cheering at the sight. They could not wait to enter the water.

The maxis stopped, and everyone got off. People looked for the best spots and were spreading their blankets, opening their chairs and umbrellas and settling in for the day. Children started playing on the beach and some people went into the water, while others just sat taking in the scenes.

The Velasquez family set their blankets on the beach, took out their picnic basket and started eating their meal. The children ate quickly because they wanted to play on the beach. Marlon and Juanita set up two beach chairs a short distance away from the Velasquez family and they strolled along the beach to the food stalls. Marlon bought bake and shark sandwiches and drinks for them both. They then walked back to their seats and dug into their lunch. They used the opportunity to continue getting to know each other.

After lunch, many people decided to take a swim. An engaging cricket match was organized. Mr. Adams also took part in the game. The game was enjoyable. The children built sandcastles, played games with each other and swam together. Then it was time to board the maxi taxis for the trip back home. Juanita and Marlon continued getting to know each other. When they were parting ways, they exchanged phone numbers and promised to communicate with each other.

A few weeks later, Juanita found a job at a restaurant. She was kept busy at work, and her free time was spent either talking to Marlon on the phone or going out with him. They grew closer with each passing day. About three months later, Juanita asked to speak with Jose and Isabella after dinner one evening. After dinner, they all sat in the living room to chat.

Juanita was a bit nervous and she played with her fingers as she cleared her throat.

"I have something that I need to tell you both", she started. "Over the last three months, Marlon and I have been spending a lot of time together. We really like each other a lot and…....." there was a long pause.

Jose and Isabella looked at each other confused. "And what?" asked Jose with a confused look on his face.

"And he wants me to move in with him in his apartment," Juanita blurted out quickly.

Jose and Isabella looked at each other in shock.

"But you just met him a few months ago. Do you think you know him well enough? asked Jose in a stern voice.

"We have learnt so much about each other and I think I'm falling in love with him," replied Juanita.

"Love!" exclaimed Isabella.

"Love takes time and I don't think you took enough time to get to know him," commented Isabella.

"He told me that he loves me, and I love him. I believe that we are right for each other and I really want to move in with him," responded Juanita.

"Well, I am your older brother and I do not think that the time is right for you to move in with Marlon or any man. You recently came to this country, you don't know your way around, you do not have real friends here and we are your only family here. You just started working and you have not saved much money yet. This is not a wise decision," answered Jose.

"You are just my older brother and you are not my father, and this is my decision to make," retorted Juanita. She got up and stormed off to the bedroom.

Isabella got up to go after her, but Jose held her back. They both conversed in Spanish about this turn of events.

Several days passed and there was visible tension between Juanita, Jose and Isabella. Juanita did not speak to either of them or did she eat dinner with them. One day, Jose, Isabella and the children returned home from a visit to the ice cream shop. When the children went into their room, they noticed that Juanita was not there and none of her things were in the room. They ran out of the room to tell their parents their observation. Both parents ran to the room to see for themselves. It was true, Juanita apparently had left the home without informing anyone of her whereabouts. Jose grabbed his cell phone and repeatedly dialled her number, but the phone just kept ringing. He left several messages but there was no reply. Isabella tried the number as well, but she also got no response. They were both worried and they barely got any sleep that night.

The next day, Isabella got a voice note from Juanita stating that she was fine and that she had moved in with Marlon and all was well. She also stated that they did not need to worry about her. Jose had requested an emergency day from work, which he was granted. He went to Juanita's workplace to have a conversation with her and he was astonished to learn that Juanita had resigned from her job a week before. Jose looked totally confused and again tried her phone, but once again there was no response. Just at that moment, a call from Isabella came through. She told him about the voice note and that he should not worry because Juanita is an adult and entitled to make her own decisions. Jose in a dazed state walked out of the restaurant and boarded a taxi to head home.

Things were going well for Juanita and Marlon. Juanita stayed home and took care of the apartment because Marlon did not want her to work. She cooked, cleaned, washed and took care of the home. Every day she got up early to make breakfast before Marlon went off to work and she also made him a hot lunch to take to work with him. In the evening, there was a fresh dinner waiting for him, as he never liked to eat the same meal twice in a row. It was his responsibility to take care of the bills and to purchase all the supplies for the home. She was not allowed to leave the house unless they were together. Juanita did not like this, but she abided by it to keep Marlon happy.

One day, after much begging from Juanita, Marlon came home early from work and they went for a stroll around the Queen's Park Savannah. They walked along holding hands and laughing and smiling with each other, just like they did when they first started dating and Juanita was really enjoying herself. She told Marlon that she wanted a snow cone, so she sat on a nearby bench while Marlon went to purchase it. At that very moment, a man sat on the same bench next to Juanita. He leaned over to her and asked her the time. Juanita glanced at her watch and told him the time.

The man replied, "Thank you. I really like your accent. Where are you from?"

"I am from Venezuela," responded Juanita.

The man answered, "I spent some time over there, where exactly are you from?"

"Really? I am from......."

At that moment, Marlon angrily grabbed Juanita's hand and yanked her off the bench. He pulled her along the path away from the man. As he passed a bin, he dumped the snow cone into it and started shouting at her.

He yelled at her, "I am the one taking care of you not that man. Who is he, your boyfriend?"

Juanita with a shocked look on her face responded, "No! I do not know him at all. He just asked me the time and we started a conversation."

"So, you think I am stupid, just like that, you and a stranger started a conversation?" shouted Marlon.

"I am telling you the truth; I do not know him!" responded Juanita.

"Stop lying!" roared Marlon as he hit her across her face.

Juanita shrieked in pain and grabbed her face. Marlon grabbed her by the arm again and pulled her to the car. He pushed her into the front passenger seat, slammed the car door and jumped into the driver's side, started the car and drove away. People standing around were in total shock about the event they just witnessed.

Juanita cried all the way home. Marlon apologised profusely to Juanita that night. She just remained silent and they went to bed in total silence. Juanita did not sleep; she knew that she needed to formulate a plan to get out of the situation as quickly as possible.

The next morning, she got up early and prepared both breakfast and lunch for Marlon as usual. Again, Marlon apologised to her. She sheepishly accepted the apology and smiled at him. He ate his breakfast, grabbed his lunch, kissed Juanita and hurried out the door. After Juanita was sure that he had left, she packed her bags and left the apartment. She did not know where she was going, but she knew that she needed to get away fast. She felt so ashamed to call either Isabella or Jose because of the manner in which she had left their home. She didn't know what to do.

She found her way to the City of Grand Bazaar, which was the nearest mall to the Velasquez's home. She sat in the Food Court and decided to call Isabella. She picked up the phone, looked for Isabella's number and hesitated. Feelings of confusion about Marlon's behaviour, the shame she felt at the Savannah, the questions about why Marlon treated her that way, what was she going to say to Isabella and Jose, would they take her back, flooded her mind and tears ran down her face. She wiped the tears and picked up the phone and looked at it for a while. She finally dialled Isabella's number and waited for the response.

Isabella was not at work that day as she had a day off. She was in the kitchen when her phone rang. She saw it was Juanita's number. She dried her hands quickly on a dish towel and answered it.

"Juanita?" responded Isabella.

There was silence on the other end of the phone.

"Juanita are you alright?" asked Isabella.

Again, there was silence on the phone.

The sound of Isabella's voice made Juanita start to cry.

"Juanita, where are you?" queried Isabella.

"Wherever you are, I will come to get you. Just tell me where you are," replied Isabella.

Juanita wiped her tears and summoned enough courage to tell Isabella where she was.

"I am at Grand Bazaar, in the Food Court," answered Juanita.

"Stay there, I am coming to get you," responded Isabella.

Isabella turned off the stove, changed her clothes quickly and left the house hurriedly to meet Juanita.

Juanita sat with her eyes glued to the glass doors of the Food Court, waiting to set her eyes on Isabella. When she saw her approaching the doors, she stood up for Isabella to see her. She ran straight to Isabella who held her arms wide open to lovingly receive Juanita. All Juanita could do was cry on Isabella's shoulder, while Isabella comforted her.

After Juanita had a good cry, Isabella asked her to tell her all the details of her experience. Isabella listened without judgement to everything she had to say. When Juanita was finished rehashing her sordid ordeal, Isabella stood up, picked up her suitcase, grabbed her hand and pulled her up.

"Let us go home," responded Isabella.

Juanita stopped her.

"Wait, what is my brother going to say? He warned me, he told me that I was not ready yet. He will be mad at me," stated Isabella.

"You are right, he did give you great advice which you turned down. He was angry when you left without a word. He was worried about you when he could not find you, but he is your brother, he will always love you even when you make mistakes. Let's go home," responded Isabella wisely. With that statement, Juanita took up her other bags and followed Isabella home.

That evening, when Jose came through the door, his eyes fell upon Juanita. He stood shocked looking at both Isabella and Juanita. He stood in place for a while, confused by the whole scene. Juanita was afraid, she also stood in place and looked at the ground. Jose then put down his bags and opened his arms wide to receive Juanita. She smiled and ran into her brother's arms and wept. They said nothing to each other, they just sat at the dining table and had a lovely family dinner.

Dear Mama,

I hope all is well with you and everyone. Everyone here is doing well. Juan and Sofia are doing extremely well in school. Juan is getting A's and B's and Sofia is getting B's for now. They love their schools and teachers.

Isabella has gotten a promotion; she is now the supervisor at the bar. They continue to treat her well. She is aiming to become the manager. I have also gotten a promotion at my job. I am a floor manager of the super-market as they have expanded the business. We are making better salaries now. This is due partly to the Migrant Registration Process that we were a part of several months ago.

The best news of all is Juanita. After the bad experience she had with the boyfriend when she moved here, she put it behind her and moved on. She is studying business part time and working, and she is handling it well. She met a really nice gentleman who has fallen in love with her. He treats her really well. He asked me for her hand in marriage and I said yes, with one condition. They are engaged at the moment but will only marry when she completes her studies in six months. They are happy together and that makes me happy.

We have saved up enough money for you and Diego to come over and spend some time with us. We are really excited about this; more details will follow about the trip soon.

As much as we miss home, Trinidad and Tobago has become our home away from home. We are indeed living a beautiful life.

Looking forward to seeing you soon.

Love,

Jose